A River

by Marc Martin

t

templar publishing

There is a river outside my window.

From where I sit, I can see it stretching into the distance in both directions.

Sometimes I imagine myself floating along the river,
swept away in a silver boat towards the horizon.

Where will it take me?

It goes through the city, under bridges and past the speeding cars that zoom by

in an endless stream of busyness.

It flows beside the factories with their machines grinding

and plumes of smoke rising into the sky.

It carries me past the farms and animals,

and moves beyond the fields that look like giant patchwork quilts.

It slides into the hills and valleys,

and I can hear the murmuring of running water...

...that grows louder

and takes me tumbling down a waterfall
taller than any building.

The river flows into the jungle,

and I can hear lots of animals –
gibbons, bats and all kinds of birds.

Deep in the jungle, it's very dark.

I can feel many eyes watching me.

As I sail through the mangroves,

the river opens up and takes me to the ocean.

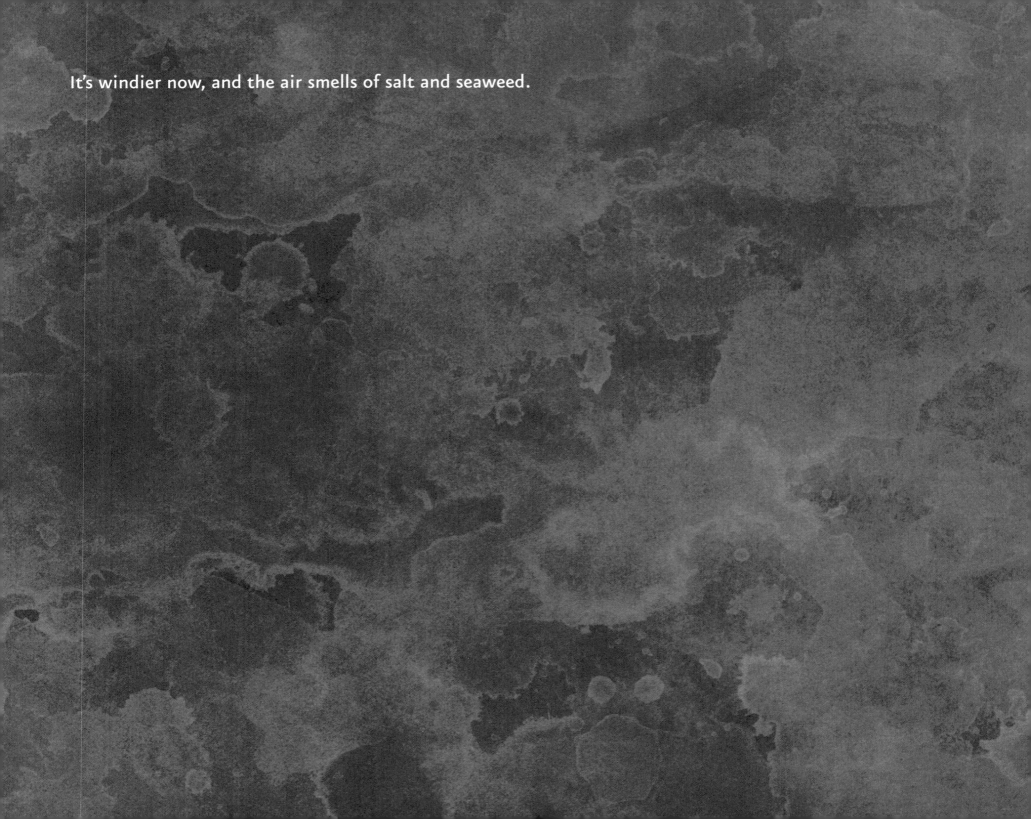

It's windier now, and the air smells of salt and seaweed.

If I peer over the edge of my boat,

I can see many fish swimming in and out of the light.

When I look up, I see clouds moving,

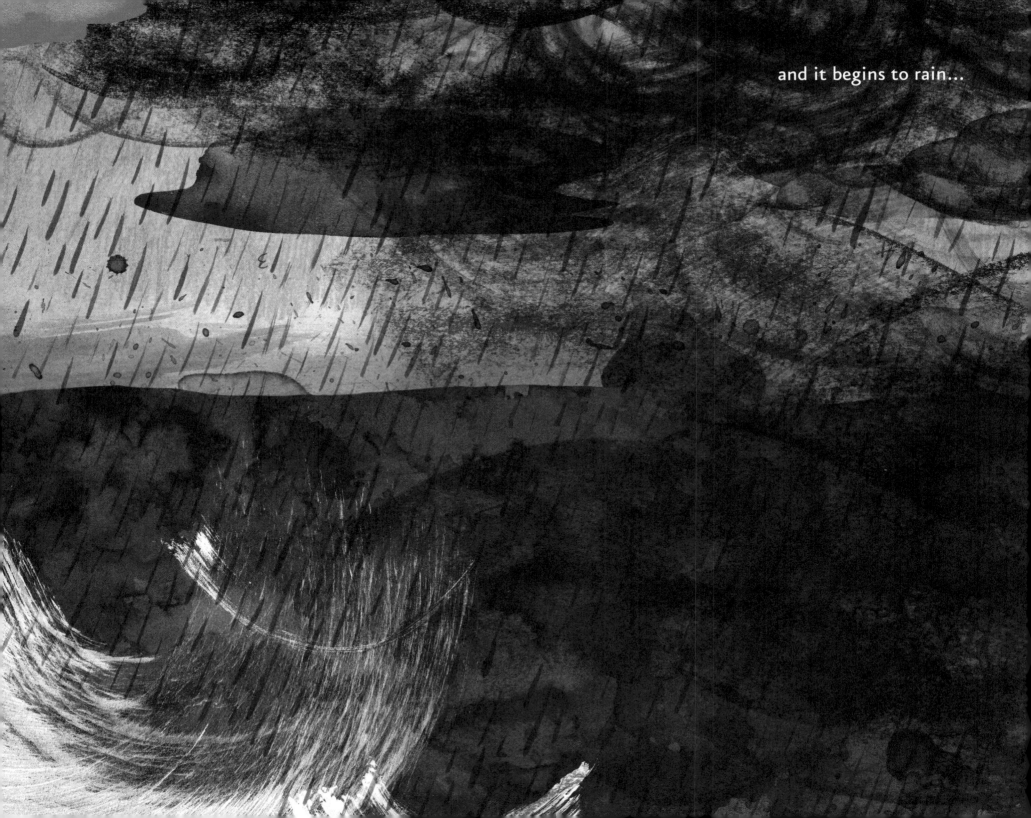

and it begins to rain…

and it's difficult to see where I am.
But I can hear raindrops on a window,

and as the clouds clear

I'm sitting in my room again,

looking through those raindrops on the glass,
and gazing out across the sleeping city.

And I think I see my silver boat,
floating in the moonlight,
drifting past my window once more.